The History of

THE FIRST MOON LANDING

Dividing Decimals

Nicole Sipe

Consultants

Lisa Ellick, M.A.
Math Specialist
Norfolk Public Schools

Pamela Estrada, M.S.Ed.
Teacher
Westminster School District

Publishing Credits

Rachelle Cracchiolo, M.S.Ed., *Publisher*
Conni Medina, M.A.Ed., *Managing Editor*
Dona Herweck Rice, *Series Developer*
Emily R. Smith, M.A.Ed., *Series Developer*
Diana Kenney, M.A.Ed., NBCT, *Content Director*
Stacy Monsman, M.A., *Editor*
Kristy Stark, M.A.Ed., *Editor*
Kevin Panter, *Graphic Designer*

Image Credits:
Front cover, pp.1, 3–4, 6–8, 10–14, 18,– 24, 27, 29, 25 (insert), courtesy NASA; p.15
Romrodphoto/Shutterstock; p.16 Claus Lunau/Science Photo Library; p.22 Maurice
Savage/Alamy; p.23 (insert) Corbis via Getty Images; p.24–25 U.S. Navy photo by Milt
Putnam; p.26 courtesy NASA, photo by Bill Taub; all other images from iStock and/or
Shutterstock.

Library of Congress Cataloging-in-Publication Data

Names: Sipe, Nicole, author.
Title: The history of the first moon landing / Nicole Sipe.
Description: Huntington Beach, CA : Teacher Created Materials, 2017. |
    Includes index. | Audience: Grades 4 to 6.
Identifiers: LCCN 2017029065 (print) | LCCN 2017032807 (ebook) | ISBN
    9781425859688 (eBook) | ISBN 9781425858223 (pbk.)
Subjects: LCSH: Project Apollo (U.S.)--History--Juvenile literature. | Space
    flight to the moon--History--Juvenile literature.
Classification: LCC TL789.8.U6 (ebook) | LCC TL789.8.U6 A581797 2017 (print)
    | DDC 629.45/4--dc23
LC record available at https://lccn.loc.gov/2017029065

Teacher Created Materials

5301 Oceanus Drive
Huntington Beach, CA 92649-1030
http://www.tcmpub.com

ISBN 978-1-4258-5822-3

© 2018 Teacher Created Materials, Inc.
Printed in China
Nordica.112019.CA21901979

Table of Contents

Mission to the Moon

The ground is soft under the **astronaut's** feet. He takes one step and then another. The dust on the ground sticks like gray chalk to the sides of his large boots. Every step he takes is in slow motion. Each step requires careful thinking. His body feels **weightless** each time he moves and even when he is still.

In the **distance**, a bright orb shines in the black velvet sky. The astronaut looks at the familiar sphere that he calls home. Earth looks so different from 238,855 miles (384,400 kilometers) away. It looks like a brilliant jewel when looking at it from the moon.

Buzz Aldrin's footprint on the moon's surface

History in the Making

The first moon landing was an important event in history. Men had already been to space. But, no one had ever landed on the moon until the U.S. Apollo 11 mission. Astronauts Neil Armstrong, Buzz Aldrin, and Michael Collins landed on the moon. The Apollo 11 mission to the moon was a big **accomplishment**. It was a victory for Americans. And, it was a victory for people all around the world.

This postage stamp honors Neil Armstrong.

NASA mathematician Katherine Johnson checked the calculations for Apollo 11's flight path to the moon.

Out to Launch

People wondered for many years what it would be like to visit the moon. Then, in 1961, President John F. Kennedy had an idea. His idea was to land a crew of people on the moon and return them safely to Earth. No other country in the world had landed on the moon. The United States would be the first.

One government group was given the job of coming up with a way to send people to the moon. This group is called the National Aeronautics and Space Administration (NASA). They were in charge of the **technology** and science of airplanes and outer space. For eight years, NASA made plans and experimented. They were focused on the goal of putting a man on the moon.

Finally, in 1969, NASA's hard work paid off. They were ready to make the **lunar** landing a reality. All they needed was to find the right crew. But, who would be ready for the important job? Who would want to be the first people on the moon?

President John F. Kennedy learns about the *Saturn* spacecraft from Dr. Wernher von Braun during a tour at Cape Canaveral.

The spacecraft used for the Apollo 11 mission is set up to launch at NASA's Kennedy Space Center.

Meet the Crew

Three men were chosen to be a part of the Apollo 11 crew. All three men were experienced astronauts. They had all flown into space before. Interestingly enough, they were all born in 1930, weighed the same amount, and were almost all the same height. They were meant to be a team!

Michael Collins

Neil Armstrong

Edwin "Buzz" Aldrin

Each astronaut had a job to do during the mission. They each had different tasks. But, each role was important to the success of the mission.

Neil Armstrong was chosen to be commander of the Apollo 11 mission. Armstrong had fallen in love with flying at a young age. He earned his pilot's license on his 16th birthday. He became a pilot even before getting his driver's license! On Apollo 11, he was the main person in charge of the spacecraft. He was also the leader of the crew. His responsibility was to make sure the crew and spacecraft were safe. He was responsible for the overall success of the mission.

official mission badge from Apollo 11

LET'S EXPLORE MATH

The combined mass of the three Apollo 11 astronauts was about 224.4 kilograms. Since each astronaut had the same mass, what was the mass of each man? Choose the correct answer, and explain your reasoning.

A. 7.48 kg   **B.** 74.8 kg   **C.** 748 kg

astronaut Buzz Aldrin inside the Lunar Module

Edwin "Buzz" Aldrin was chosen to be the Lunar **Module** pilot. Buzz got his nickname from his younger sister. She could not say "brother," so it came out as "Buzzer." The name stuck! He legally changed his name to Buzz in 1988.

Aldrin's job on Apollo 11 was to **navigate** to and land on the moon. During the mission, he and Armstrong would board a smaller, special spacecraft—the Lunar Module *Eagle*—to get to the moon. This spacecraft was made especially for a moon mission.

Michael Collins was chosen to be the Command Module pilot. While his two partners **explored** the moon, his job was to **orbit** and keep things under control on the main spacecraft. Some people might think his job was not very glamorous. After all, he did not get to walk on the moon! But, it was an important job. He helped make the trip a success. He wrote about that success in 1976 in a children's book called *Flying to the Moon: An Astronaut's Story.*

LET'S EXPLORE MATH

Suppose that paperback copies of Collins's book can be purchased for $8.

1. How many dimes are in $8? Write a division equation to show your thinking.

2. How many pennies are in $8? Write a division equation to show your thinking.

3. How are your answers related to $8?

Michael Collins

The Apollo crew performs tests in the Command Module six days before launch.

Meet the Craft

The Apollo 11 mission used a rocket called *Saturn V*. (*V* is the Roman numeral for *five*.) This rocket was built to send people to the moon. When it was full of fuel, it weighed about 6.2 million pounds (2.8 million kilograms). That is the weight of about 15 adult blue whales! The rocket was 363 feet (111 meters) tall. That is about 60 ft. (18 m) taller than the Statue of Liberty in New York. It was one powerful rocket!

Apollo 11 had three spacecraft. The first was the Command Module *Columbia*. It was where the men lived. *Columbia* was the size of a large car. It was a snug fit, but it had everything they needed. It had equipment, food, clothing, and bathrooms.

The second spacecraft was the Service Module. It carried oxygen, water, and power for *Columbia*.

The third spacecraft was the Lunar Module *Eagle*. *Eagle* would take the astronauts to the moon, land on its surface, and bring them back to the *Columbia*.

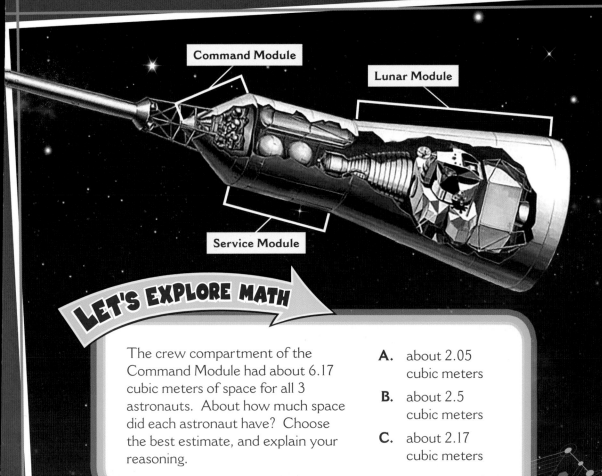

LET'S EXPLORE MATH

The crew compartment of the Command Module had about 6.17 cubic meters of space for all 3 astronauts. About how much space did each astronaut have? Choose the best estimate, and explain your reasoning.

A. about 2.05 cubic meters

B. about 2.5 cubic meters

C. about 2.17 cubic meters

Apollo 11 launches on the morning of July 16, 1969.

3...2...1...
Liftoff!

It was a clear, sunny morning on July 16, 1969. History was about to be made! Apollo 11 was set to launch from Kennedy Space Center in Florida.

The astronauts ate a breakfast of steak and scrambled eggs. They had toast, coffee, and orange juice, too. Then, they took their seats in the spacecraft. Everything was checked and double-checked with Mission Control Center. At last, Apollo 11 was ready to go!

With a rumble and a roar, it launched at 9:32 a.m. Millions of people around the world watched the launch on TV. Some even saw it in person. It was a thrilling sight!

Apollo 11 had to fly very fast to escape Earth's **gravity**. The spacecraft traveled about 25,000 mi. (40,234 km) per hour. That is about 7 mi. (11 km) per second, or 32 times faster than the speed of sound! But, it did not travel at that rate the entire **journey**. The crew adjusted the speed once they made it out of Earth's **atmosphere**.

Members of a school science club like to eat the same breakfast as the Apollo 11 astronauts. The orange juice comes in 1.5 liter bottles. Each member receives a 0.3 liter serving. How many members can be served from one bottle of juice? Use the model to find and explain your solution.

$$1.5 \div 0.3 = \boxed{}$$

NASA Launch Control Center, Cape Canaveral, Florida

This computer-generated illustration shows the path and stages of the Apollo 11 mission.

The Apollo 11 mission was not a direct flight to the moon. It happened in stages. First, it orbited Earth one and a half times. When the spacecraft was in the right position, the crew got a "go" for the next stage—to the moon!

On July 20, the Apollo 11 crew reached the moon. It had taken them four days.

The Mighty Moon

In the night sky, the moon looks rather close to Earth, right? Well, it is not! The moon is actually very far from Earth. It is an average of 238,855 mi. (384,399 km) away.

That distance isn't always the same. The moon does not orbit Earth in a perfect circle. It actually orbits in an **ellipse**. An ellipse is like an oval. When the moon is closest to Earth, it is about 225,623 mi. (363,105 km) away. When the moon is farthest from Earth, it is about 252,088 miles (405,696 km) away. You would have to stack about 30 Earths, end to end, to reach that distance. That means a journey to the moon is a long trip!

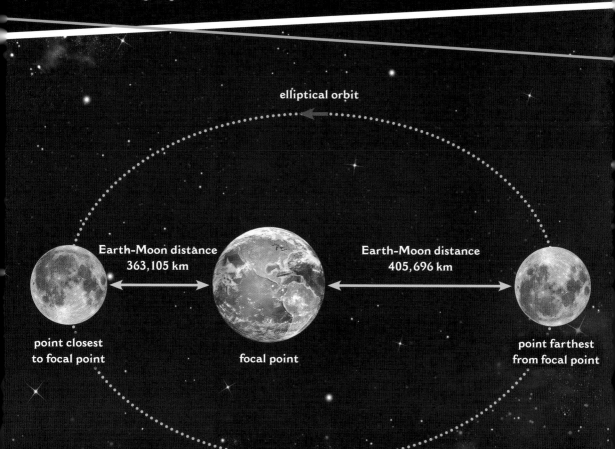

elliptical orbit

Earth-Moon distance
363,105 km

Earth-Moon distance
405,696 km

point closest
to focal point

focal point

point farthest
from focal point

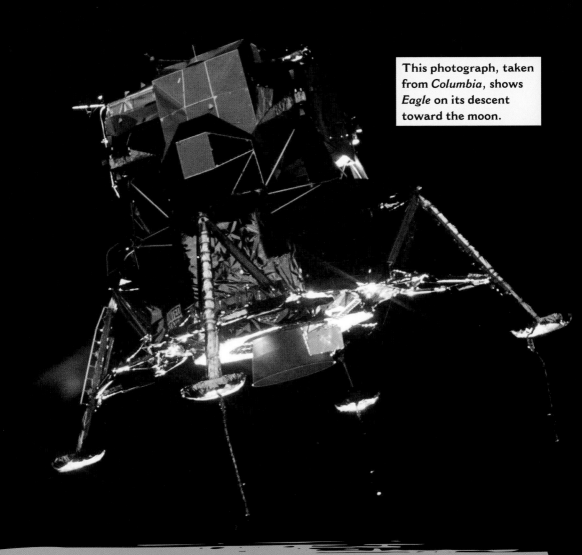

This photograph, taken from *Columbia*, shows *Eagle* on its descent toward the moon.

The *Eagle* Has Landed

It was the morning of July 20, 1969. Armstrong and Aldrin climbed into the *Eagle* spacecraft. Their **destination**: the moon! Collins stayed on *Columbia*. After hours of running through checklists and about 100 hours into the flight, *Eagle* separated from *Columbia*.

"The *Eagle* has wings," Armstrong said.

The Apollo 11 mission did not go exactly as planned. The men had planned to land on a specific spot in the Sea of Tranquility. The Sea of Tranquility is not a body of water. It is a dark spot on the moon. This spot was chosen because it was thought to be a smooth place to land. But, it was not as smooth as they thought! The landing area looked like a jagged boulder field. Landing on rocks would destroy *Eagle*. *Eagle* was fragile and covered with a paper-thin skin.

Neil Armstrong

The astronauts had to choose another place to land. With less than a minute's worth of fuel left, the astronauts found a smooth area. It was about 4 mi. (6 km) away from where they had originally planned to land. Finally, *Eagle* touched down on the moon.

LET'S EXPLORE MATH

Aldrin and Armstrong stood next to each other in the cockpit of *Eagle* to control it during ascent and descent. The width of the cockpit was about 4.3 meters. How much standing space did each astronaut have? Use the model to find and explain your solution.

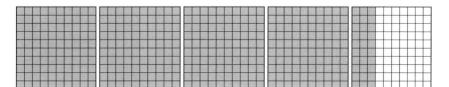

$$4.3 \div 2 = \square$$

"The *Eagle* has landed," Armstrong reported.

The astronauts put on their bulky space suits. It was time to leave *Eagle*. Armstrong opened a hatch on the outside of the spacecraft. The hatch contained a small TV camera. Anyone with a TV anywhere in the world could watch what was taking place.

Armstrong slowly climbed down the ladder of *Eagle*. He stepped onto the surface of the moon. About 530 million people all over the world watched and heard as Armstrong announced his first steps on the moon, "That's one small step for man, one giant leap for mankind."

Buzz Aldrin descends to the surface of the moon from the Lunar Module.

Buzz Aldrin poses while Neil Armstrong takes a photo.

Twenty minutes later, Aldrin climbed out next. He stepped onto the moon. He looked around at the rocky, gray **landscape**.

"Beautiful view!" Aldrin exclaimed. "Magnificent sight out here. Magnificent **desolation**."

Walking on the moon was not like walking on Earth. It took the astronauts time to learn how to move around. The gravity on the moon is one-sixth what it is on Earth. Because of this, the astronauts moved slowly and felt as light as feathers. They had fun figuring out how to move in this unusual environment.

The astronauts explored the moon for two and a half hours. During that time, they picked up 47 lbs. (21.3 kg) of moon rock and soil to bring back to Earth. They set up **experiments** and took pictures.

Armstrong and Aldrin planted an American flag on the moon. They also left behind a stainless-steel **plaque**. The plaque reads, "Here men from the planet Earth first set foot upon the moon. July 1969 A.D. We came in peace for all mankind." President Richard Nixon called the astronauts on the telephone. He told them, "For one priceless moment in the whole history of man, all the people on this Earth are truly one." This was the longest long-distance telephone call in history!

After they had completed their assigned tasks, it was time for the astronauts to climb back into *Eagle*. Aldrin went in first, followed by Armstrong. They safely stored their rock and soil samples in the spacecraft. They took off their spacesuits. Then, they ate dinner and tried to get some sleep. In a few hours, they would start the long trip back home.

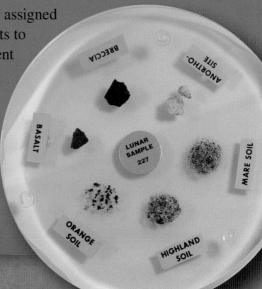

lunar rock samples

LET'S EXPLORE MATH

Aldrin and Armstrong collected about 21.3 kilograms of rock and soil samples. Imagine that each of them carried the same amount back to *Eagle*. How much would each astronaut have carried? Estimate and then calculate your answer. Compare your estimate with the actual answer.

President Richard Nixon speaks with the astronauts of Apollo 11 while they are on the moon.

Buzz Aldrin salutes the U.S. flag.

Back to Earth

Splash! On July 24, Apollo 11 re-entered Earth's atmosphere. It splashed down into the Pacific Ocean as planned. The astronauts were back on Earth! The mission was complete. Men had walked on the moon and made it safely back to Earth. The trip had taken 8 days, 3 hours, 18 minutes, and 35 seconds. The astronauts had traveled nearly 1 million mi. (1.6 million km).

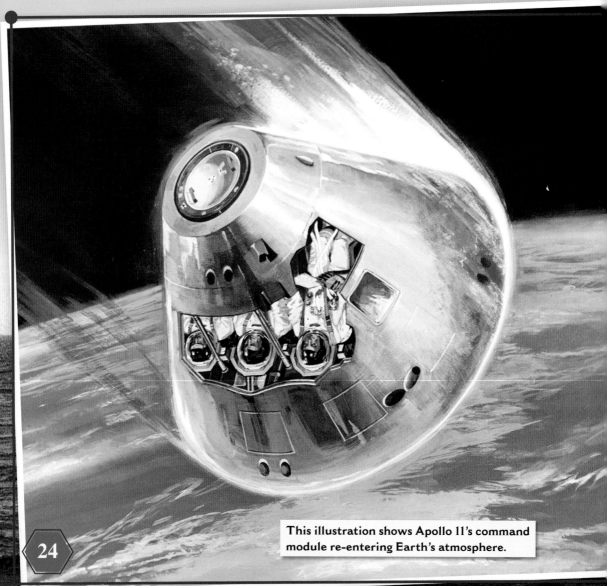

This illustration shows Apollo 11's command module re-entering Earth's atmosphere.

Before they could celebrate, the astronauts needed to get out of their spacecraft and onto dry land. Armstrong, Aldrin, and Collins climbed aboard an aircraft carrier named the USS *Hornet*. The three men were then sent to **quarantine**. This was to make sure they didn't bring back any germs or diseases from the moon.

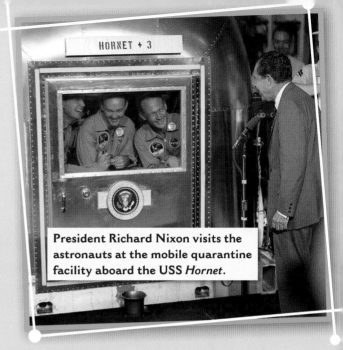

President Richard Nixon visits the astronauts at the mobile quarantine facility aboard the USS *Hornet*.

President Nixon was onboard the ship. He congratulated the astronauts on a job well done. He spoke to them from outside their quarantine chamber.

"As a result of what you've done, the world's never been closer together," President Nixon said. "We can reach for the stars just as you have." The brave men were heroes.

USS *Hornet*

The astronauts wave to the crowd lining the parade route.

The astronauts spent 21 days in quarantine. Then, they were free to go home. Now, the celebration could really begin! One of the biggest celebrations took place in New York City. The astronauts were greeted with a parade. A shower of **ticker tape** and confetti rained from the sky. Armstrong, Aldrin, and Collins rode in a car and waved at the cheering crowd. It was the largest parade in the city's history!

The Apollo 11 mission opened the door to more explorations to the moon. After that historic event, there were five more American lunar missions. A total of 12 astronauts have gone to the moon and seen its wonder.

NASA has more moon missions planned for the future. By 2020, NASA hopes to send another crew to the moon. This time, the mission will be to set up a base where people can live. This base will be a launch site for missions to Mars and other places in space. One day, we will read about the first people to land on Mars!

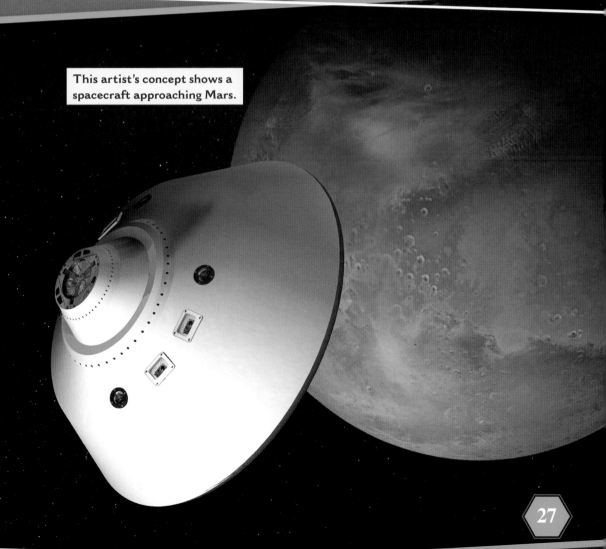

This artist's concept shows a spacecraft approaching Mars.

⚙️ Problem Solving

Even astronauts need to eat! For the crew of Apollo 11, their special diets started in the days before the historic flight. Each food item had to be carefully measured according to strict guidelines. A personal chef prepared food for the astronauts.

Imagine that you are the personal chef for the astronauts in the days before liftoff. Complete the table and answer the questions to make sure your meal plan measures up.

1. Insert decimal points in the numbers in the last column of the table to make them correct.

2. As a special treat, sherbet is served for dessert. There are 680.4 grams of sherbet. Each serving must be 113.4 grams. How many servings can be prepared? Explain your reasoning.

3. A pantry on the craft is stocked with extra food in case the flight is extended due to bad weather or other reasons. There are 226.8 grams of chicken salad. If the 3 astronauts equally share the chicken salad, how much will each of them get? Explain your reasoning.

4. The pantry has 3 servings of cheddar cheese. Each serving is 56.7 grams. Estimate the total mass of the cheddar cheese. Explain your reasoning.

Selected Pre-Flight Menu Items

Food Item	Total Mass (g)	Number of Servings Needed	Mass of Each Serving (g)
strained grapefruit	340.2	3	1134
breakfast steak	510.3	3	1701
butter	113.4	12	945

Glossary

accomplishment—something done or achieved

astronaut—a trained person who travels to space

atmosphere—a layer that surrounds Earth

desolation—a state of being deserted

destination—a place to go

distance—the amount of space between two objects

ellipse—an oval shape

experiments—scientific tests performed to make a discovery

explored—learned by doing

gravity—the force of attraction between two objects

journey—trip from one place to another

landscape—an area of land that has a certain quality or appearance

lunar—of or relating to the moon

module—a set of parts to make a whole

navigate—to travel on, over, or through

orbit—to travel around something in a curved path

plaque—a flat piece of metal with writing on it usually presented in honor of a person or event

quarantine—to keep away from others to prevent the spread of disease

technology—machines and digital devices used to solve problems

ticker tape—a paper strip on which messages are recorded

weightless—having no weight or seeming to have no weight

Index

Answer Key

Let's Explore Math

page 9:

B; Explanations will vary but may include using estimation and multiplication to show that 7.48 × 3 is a little over 21 kg, so that is too low; 748 × 3 is over 2,100 kg, so that is too high. Only 74.8 is reasonable since 75 × 3 is 225 kg.

page 11:

1. 80 dimes; 8 ÷ 0.10 = 80

2. 800 pennies; 8 ÷ 0.01 = 800

3. Answers will vary but may include that 80 is 10 times greater than 8 and 800 is 100 times greater than 8.

page 13:

A; Explanations will vary but may include that 3 groups of 2 is 6, and 3 groups of 5 hundredths (0.05) is 15 hundredths (0.15), making 2.05 the closest estimate.

page 15:

5 members; Models should show 5 groups of 0.3. Example:

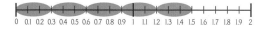

page 19:

2.15 m; Models will vary but should include labeling 2 whole hundredths grids for each astronaut, and labeling 15 of the 30 hundredths for each astronaut.

page 22:

Estimates will vary but should be between 10 and 11; 10.65 kg; Comparisons will vary but may include that the estimate is close to the actual answer.

Problem Solving

1. 113.4; 170.1; 9.45

2. 6 servings; Explanations will vary but may include using models, equations, or estimation to divide 680.4 by 113.4, or to multiply 113.4 by 6.

3. 75.6 g; Explanations will vary, but may include using models, equations, or estimation to divide 226.8 by 3.

4. Estimates will vary, but should be between 165 g and 180 g; Explanations will vary, but may include rounding 56.7 and muliplying by 3.